THAT LOVE NONSENSE

Also by Alexandria Blaelock

MS BLAELOCK'S BOOKS
Stress Free Dinner Parties
Signature Wardrobe Planning
Holistic Personal Finance
Minimally Viable Housekeeping

SHORT STORIES
Alma's Grace
Balancing the Book
Fate in Your Hands
Kiss of Death
Lady of the Looking Glass
Life in the Security Directorate
Long Weekend in the Snow
Love in the Security Directorate
Needy Bitch
Payton's Run
Phoenix Child
Shining Star
Ship in a Bottle
Simone Says Hands in the Air
The Guardian's Vigil
The Life and Death of Carmelita Basingstoke

That Love Nonsense

A SHORT NOVEL

ALEXANDRIA BLAELOCK

BlueMere Books
MELBOURNE, AUSTRALIA

For permission requests, please contact
enquiries@bluemerebooks.com.

Ordering Information:
Discounts are available on quantity purchases. For details, contact
orders@bluemerebooks.com.

That Love Nonsense/Alexandria Blaelock
hardback ISBN: 978-1-925749-34-2
paperback ISBN: 978-1-925749-35-9
digital ISBN: 978-1-925749-36-6

Book Layout © BookDesignTemplates.com

For Unicorn John

$$1$$

Daniel glanced up to see where the tram had stopped. The commuters in the centre of the carriage seethed and rearranged themselves like a school of fish as people disembarked and others climbed in.

A space opened up, and just for an instant, a woman stood alone in its centre. Her back was to him, but the dark, fitted, retro-styled skirt suit she wore highlighted her trim figure.

She was standing arms folded, balancing evenly on her slightly spaced legs, riding the turbulence like a high-heeled surfer.

For an instant, he imagined her, head thrown back, riding him.

And then, as she abruptly turned her head, just in the nick of time to avoid being hit in the face by some guy's backpack, as an old, black and white comic book superhero come to life.

Travelling incognito as her mild-mannered alter ego of course.

He willed her to turn around and show him the cateye glasses and dark lipstick he was convinced she was wearing.

He almost stood up to fight through the crowd to her to offer his seat, though of course by the time he reached her, the seat would be taken.

The tram lurched, and with a metallic squeal of wheels started moving again. He imagined her smiling slightly as she rocked; swaying sexily without stumbling.

Someone in the aisle behind him staggered, setting off a cascade of nudging and bumping that surged down the carriage like a wave.

He decided she'd ridden it out with barely a nudge.

Someone nearby farted silently, and he half coughed, half retched as the smell hit him.

At least being winter, he didn't have to worry too much about antiperspirant failures as well.

Daniel pointed his nose toward the window and was astonished to see the woman's face blurrily reflected in its smeary surface.

Incredible.

No cateye glasses, but she was wearing dark lipstick.

The kind of square face that might be handsome on a man, but generally considered unfortunate on a woman. Particularly one wearing that kind of a short masculine hairstyle, such a pale blond it was almost invisible from his distance.

It gave him the idea she was the kind of person who lived her life on her own terms.

But more intriguingly, her eyes were closed.

Perhaps so familiar with every tilt and swing of the journey she could take it eyes closed, without the assistance of a grab bar or handle. Or so confident she could read the movement through her feet she didn't need to watch.

Not something he could do.

Not that he'd ever tried.

Though, not being very tall, she probably couldn't reach the grab handles anyway.

Then again, maybe she was one of those people who could sleep standing up. Like a bird, half her brain always turned on.

He'd been on this tram route for years, how was it possible he'd never seen her before?

Then again, even if she was the kind of woman who kept a nice, neat daily routine, he didn't. It wasn't likely they'd caught the 18:06 on the same day before.

And even if they had, it was a strange coincidental circumstance he'd noticed her in the first place. Front on, wearing something less distinctive, he probably wouldn't have.

Not that he was looking for a personal entanglement that lasted longer than a couple of hours anyway, but aside from being of the female persuasion, she wasn't his type.

And yet...

He was curious.

The tram juddered to a halt, and the doors clanked opened with a groan.

His pocket buzzed, and Steve's text reminded him of Mariel's birthday party. He cursed under his breath as he realised this was the stop for the restaurant.

He bolted out of the seat.

"Excuse me," he said pushing past passengers, "excuse me," as he pushed his way through to the exit, "excuse me," as he forced his way out the doors just as they closed.

Almost catching his ankle as he dived for the kerb

He bent over, breathing heavily, worn out by battling off the tram.

And exhausted by the idea of having to spend the evening celebrating best mate Steve's wife's birthday with their family and friends.

Still, there'd be free booze.

But now, his imagination hooked by the idea of his tram surfing comic book superhero, he wanted a slightly different end to his evening than getting drunk and going home alone.

And given those two, and their perpetual rose-coloured matchmaking attempts, they'd have lined up one of their single friends for him already.

But maybe this time, she'd be okay.

2

Norah pushed her way off the tram and wondered once again why she'd agreed to go to Mariel's birthday dinner.

She knew, despite her begging, one of Steve's friends would be earmarked for her.

What was it with married people, that they couldn't leave well enough alone.

Yes, technically she was single.

But Nick had been the love of her life, even if he was a better husband dead than he was alive.

You don't just pack up and move on when the man of your dreams wastes away in front of you. You need time to grieve, time to come to terms with life not going according to plan.

Time to recover from the physically and mentally exhausting effort of keeping your shit together in front of him, and everyone else.

Every single goddamned second of the goddamned day.

As he sickened and died.

At the funeral.

In the aftermath.

Trying to regain your physical and mental strength as your friends abandon you one by one because they have no idea what to say to you.

And you make them feel bad for being happy and laughing.

Not deliberately, of course, but just by being around reminding them of what they have to lose.

What you've already lost.

Norah gave herself a mental shake.

Maybe she *had* waited too long to get back in the dating game, but she'd been on so many awkwardly bad dates by this point, it seemed she just didn't know how to date any more.

Surely it wasn't possible that every single uncommitted straight man on the planet was a self-absorbed, narcissistic loser.

Was it?

Easier to stick to boyfriends with batteries and not worry about finding a live one.

She was too old for a "boyfriend" anyway.

And not entirely convinced a "man-friend" was a viable alternative.

Though sometimes it would be nice to have something else living and breathing in her apartment.

Maybe what she really needed was a dog.

Or a cat, they were a bit more independent than dogs.

Wildlife killers that they were.

She stood in the darkness across the road, crazy cat lady in waiting, looking at the brightly lit restaurant.

Inside, smiling birthday girl Mariel was standing by a wood-effect melamine table, already laid for the meal. She was the centre of attention, as usual, Champagne glass in hand laughing and talking with her friends. Her hands gesturing, hair flicking this way and that as she looked at whoever was speaking.

The whitewashed walls were strung with flashing strings of tiny LED lights, and some kind of recent music was playing.

Norah thought she recognised the singer's voice, but not the song.

Someone carrying takeout bags pushed the door open and exited in a wave of noise, followed by the perfume of fried garlic.

She recognised that this moment, her outside watching them inside, was like the opening scene of a Hallmark Christmas movie. And if it was, she'd be the one finding love and the Spirit of Christmas.

Though this Friday night was nowhere near Christmas.

Did Hallmark make Christmas in July movies?

Probably not, not the right thing.

By this point, she was so used to being alone, she wasn't sure she could handle that number of people at the same time anyway.

She was about to turn and walk away when Mariel looked up.

Her face broke into an enormous smile, and she walked towards the door as if she knew Norah was about to bail.

And of course she did, because they'd been best friends since kinder. They'd shared everything, even for a short time, a boyfriend, way back before they'd met Nick and Steve clubbing.

Norah forced a smile onto her face and walked across the road. Mariel pushed the door, open, grabbed her hand and pulled her into the restaurant, and then a tight hug.

"You made it!"

Norah scrunched her face up and smiled, doing the little bouncy huggy dancey thing she was far from feeling, "yay, I made it."

She pulled back as soon as Mariel loosened her grip, pulled a tiny package from her bag and offered it up to her friend "Happy Birthday."

Mariel hugged her again, "you shouldn't have," then ripped the package open, stuffing the paper into a pocket. She examined the jewelled spider brooch closely, "I love it!" she said, and pinned it haphazardly to the collar of her shirt.

"Now come with me, I want you to meet someone."

Norah groaned and glanced at her watch.

"No. No, it's not like that. You'll love him."

Norah doubted it, but decided it probably wouldn't be too hard to ditch him and make it home in time to watch a Q&A repeat on iview.

"Let me get a drink first, I have the feeling I'm going to need it."

"No need, there's table service."

"I'm sure there is, but I need it now."

"I'll come with."

"No need, I promise I'll be back before you know it."

She slipped away when Mariel's attention was stolen by another guest.

Odd how often being alone and unnoticed in a crowded room can be one of the most comfortable things.

3

Daniel couldn't believe it when he recognised his tram surfing comic book superhero stranding at the bar.

Well, not her *per se*, but the shape of her back, the tilt of her head, her loose-limbed waiting stance.

And her pencil skirt clad *derrière*.

Except now he could see her clearly.

Close up.

But.

Now she was right here, in the flesh within touching distance, he was a little reluctant to approach her.

Her actuality could never be as enticing as his imagination, could it?

The choice was taken away from him as some guy bumped him on the way past, and he was propelled towards her, almost but not quite missing her.

He knocked her elbow as she was raising her glass to drink.

Her backpack detecting superpowers kicked in, and she pushed the glass out in front of her as she curved her body back and away from it.

The red liquid surged out toward her, but missed, splashing on the floor instead.

He winced as she turned to look at him, expecting her to rebuke him for his carelessness.

And as she turned, he saw that her hair was not pale blond, but white.

Snow white.

He smothered a smile.

She was older than he'd thought, but she moved with a young, fluid, gracefulness.

Like a dancer.

Or perhaps a coloured martial arts belt holder.

Was the white hair a fashion thing, or had she suffered some kind of trauma and gone white overnight?

He was intrigued.

But after glancing at him, she merely licked her fingers and turned away again as if she found him unworthy of her attention.

She was focused on the glass, not anyone nearby.

What the hell?

He gestured to get the barman's attention. "Beer," he gestured at the woman, "another whatever of those for the lady, and a clean-up on aisle nine."

She turned back, "don't bother, I've drunk half of it anyway."

"I don't want you to look back on this evening and think I ruined it for you."

She snorted, and downed the rest of the glass, "it's probably already ruined, but not by you."

As a young man arrived with a mop, she took a step forward out of his way and placed her glass on the counter. Seconds later, the boy walked away, and she stepped back and away from Daniel.

He knew she was halfway to brushing him off, that he should leave it at that and beat a retreat. But he'd never been so quickly and thoroughly disregarded before.

And his feelings were a little hurt.

He took a step towards her, close to enough to catch the light, fresh floral scent she was wearing. It was a little old fashioned, roses and something else, a bit like his garden in Spring.

Resting his right foot on the bar, he leaned his elbow on the counter. Plenty of room for her to get away if she wanted to, but enough of a barrier to slow her down. "Why's that then?"

The barman arrived with the drinks. Daniel took his and gestured at hers with the bottle as he raised it to his lips and took the first blessed mouthful of beer.

She frowned at the drink, then at him, then shrugged and reached out with both hands for the glass.

"Dutch courage," she said, raising the glass to him in salute, and took a sip.

He couldn't help but notice her wedding ring.

He nodded and tilted his in reply.

A little disappointed, yet prepared to back off and let her go. "Are you here for Mariel's birthday party too?" she asked.

A lifeline.

Though now he'd seen the ring, he wasn't sure he wanted it.

But who's to say that a married woman might not be a better option than being thrown into a hyena pack of young single women.

No pressure. A measure of safety.

He nodded.

"Look, this is a bit of a cheek, but I know she's got some single guy here to fix me up with. Would you just sit and chat with me for a couple of hours to keep her at bay?"

He nodded at her ring, "but aren't you married?"

She frowned and held up her left hand to look at the ring for a few seconds before taking a sip of her drink. "Yes and no."

There was so much there he wanted to know, but he just cocked an eyebrow, and let the silence between them expand.

Clearly upset, in a kind of deep bruised way, she closed her eyes and tilted her face towards the ceiling.

He thought maybe she'd forgotten where she was, or what the question was.

But after a moment, she said, "he died."

And Daniel felt like a jerk. "I'm sorry."

She smiled a tight, straight-lipped smile, "ah. It was a while back, but, you know?"

"I can guess."

"Anyway, they haven't run out of guys to set me up with yet, and the last few guys were a disaster."

He snorted.

"And not that I'm looking, but dating sites aren't any better, and I feel like I had my chance, and it's just time to let all that love nonsense go."

Daniel swapped his leaning leg and took another sip of beer as he thought about what she'd said.

And wondered if he was the guy they'd organised for her.

Whether love was the kind of nonsense you could let go.

What she might be like, alone, in a different situation.

"Lord knows I've had enough bad blind dates myself," he said, "do you want to avoid all that love nonsense and blow this joint?"

She laughed, not quite throwing her head back, but tilting it enough to remind him he'd already imagined her, head thrown back, in a more intimate setting.

And reignite his curiosity.

4

Norah took a gulp of her Campari, not quite believing she'd said all that stuff, let alone he'd suggested they leave together.

But the truth was, she didn't want to be in that restaurant with Mariel and Steve. They were too happy.

As they should be, but the three of them should've been four, and even after all this time, she still found it hard to see them together without seeing the space where Nick should've been.

They had each other, had moved on. Leaving Nick, and by extension her, in the past behind them.

They meant well, but living with the ghost of her dead husband still seemed a better option than moving on without him.

Then again, this man she'd just spilled her guts to was a friend of someone she knew. Probably not a serial killer, probably safe to leave with.

Probably.

She might be widowed, but she didn't have a death wish.

She gave him a quick look up and down.

He was tall, clean-shaven, with neatly trimmed short blond hair.

Just the way she liked it.

Quite handsome, if a bit young, in a well-fitted suit and tie. She could just see the edge of a shiny silver coloured cuff link inside his jacket sleeve.

His black lace-up oxford shoes looked to be well-polished leather.

Was it reasonable to assume that if he took such good care of his clothes and appearance, he'd at least take the minimum of care with her?

Or was that asking a bit much in this day and age?

Either way, he'd probably take a nicely timed and well-spoken hint and leave her very shortly after they left the restaurant anyway.

In her recent experience, young men didn't have the attention span, let alone the stamina for anything approaching what she'd be looking for. They were all ten minutes max.

Assuming she was looking at all. Which she wasn't.

But he was neat and clean, wearing proper clothes.

She could give him five minutes, just to see.

"I might leave with you if I knew your name."

He snorted. "Is that really all it takes? I'm Daniel," he held his hand out to her.

"Norah," she said, taking it and giving it one firm shake.

"Shall we?" he asked.

She gulped the last of her drink, partly to be polite and partly for the courage she'd mentioned earlier and slid the glass onto the counter.

Then smoothed the front of her jacket down, "ready as I'll ever be."

He abandoned his drink without another sip, "I'm right behind you."

She smothered a nervous giggle, "I feel like I'm a teenager again, sneaking out of my parent's house to go clubbing."

He smiled, "no way mate. We have to at least say goodbye to the birthday girl, and then we'll walk out openly like grown-ups."

"I suppose they'd add up the numbers and guess we'd left together anyway."

She took her phone from her bag and walked over to Mariel before tucking it back in, Daniel a step behind her.

"I'm sorry Mariel," she said, "some thing's come up, and I have to go."

She gave Mariel a quick kiss on the cheek and gestured behind her, "Daniel here's going to give me a lift."

Mariel looked like she'd been hit over the head by a giant, tightly stuffed toy bear, "but..."

Daniel stepped forward and kissed her cheek as well, "uh, happy birthday Mariel. I'm not sure I'll make it back, so you have a great night."

"But..."

Almost as one, they turned and walked away.

Norah looked back and gave the stunned Mariel a little wave before pulling the restaurant door open and walking through it.

Then scurrying further down the street to a point where they would be invisible to those left behind in the restaurant.

"Thanks Daniel," she said as he caught up, "I can take it from here."

He laughed, "and what are you going to tell Mariel when she calls you tomorrow?"

"Aahhh, I'll think of something by then."

"And aren't you at all worried about what I might tell Steve we got up to when he calls?"

"Well, it's been a long time since high school, so I expect you don't need to brag about your imaginary prowess. I'd hope you'd be discreet."

He bent at the waist to lean down and look in her eyes, "that's more of a gamble than I'd have expected from a woman like yourself?"

She stood a little taller, assuming he was referring to her age "like myself? And what exactly would a woman like myself be like?"

He smiled as if he was expecting exactly that reaction, "you're well dressed in a conservative kind of way. I'd have expected you to want a little more control over the situation."

She tried to suppress her returning smile, "well if I don't answer the phone when she calls, the first person she'll suspect is you anyway."

He smiled back, "true enough." He reached out and pulled her hand through the crook of his elbow. "If I'm getting the blame anyway, it would be irresponsible to let you go without at least making sure you ate. Especially when you've just sunk a couple of cocktails."

Norah tried to pull her hand back, and almost tripped over her feet, "seems I don't have much choice."

He smiled, "I'm just taking care of my friend's wife's friend."

She growled, but he merely smiled. "There's a Chinese nearby that's not too bad."

"Fine."

He patted the hand he'd trapped and took a step, making her skip to catch up.

"I have to tell you a secret," he said.

"What? You're a serial killer?"

"No, you'd be my first."

She snorted, "first in a long line no doubt."

"Naturally. But no, I think I might be your blind date."

"Oh for crying out loud. What am I supposed to do now?"

5

Daniel laughed. Despite her protestation, she seemed to take the news with reasonably good grace. "I should also tell you I caught the tram, so my car's not nearby," he added.

"Well, that at least is not a problem. I can get a cab."

"We'll see."

He wasn't sure how he wanted the night to end.

But his tram surfing comic book superhero had slipped through a hole in the fabric of space and time, and incredibly, he had her to himself for a couple of hours.

And if she disappeared back through it again after that, well, at least he'd met her.

But he wasn't going to let her leave him early, that was for sure.

And if she stayed, well tomorrow was a whole new day.

Right now, he was going to dive deep and immerse himself in the moment.

Make it the longest night of his life, banking every moment to think about later.

Whatever happened, she was easily the most fascinating person he'd met in a long time.

Hopefully not the serial pepper-spraying kind of woman.

6

Norah matched his sauntering pace for a few steps, then paused, "do you think maybe we should go somewhere further away where we're less likely to be found out?"

"Somewhere more crowded with lots of witnesses?"

"Well that too, but I think Mariel would be hurt if she saw us on her way back to her car."

He stopped walking and turned to face her, or look over the top of her head at someone younger and prettier.

"That's a good point. Catch the tram back to town, or closer to my place?"

She froze for a moment, thinking maybe the mention of his place was a suggestion they skip eating out and head straight there.

Where he would probably steal her credit cards and empty her bank accounts.

Ah, that's right.

They were already empty - cancer treatment isn't cheap.

A gust of wind blew up, ruffling his hair and enveloping her in whatever spicy cologne he was wearing.

She noticed the heat of his body reaching out towards her across the space between them, pressing against her face and chest.

Making her aware of the strange, comforting feeling of not being alone, a feeling she'd forgotten existed.

She closed her eyes against the need to be wrapped in someone's hot, hard body. To feel their strength and share their space. To bear their weight.

No. Not anyone.

Daniel.

Singly, and specifically, and only Daniel.

Wrapped in his hot, hard, spice-scented body. Held in his strong arms. To inhale his breath as he lowered himself into her.

After only five minutes.

Well, more like half an hour.

But, was all that love nonsense really nonsense?

Or was this just lust and animal magnetism?

His closeness made her feel things she thought she'd lost along with Nick.

Daniel's heat thawed her heart a little.

His dry humour made her laugh.

The touch of his skin made hers tingle and her hair stand on end.

The smell of his cologne made her dizzy.

And he hadn't even made a pass at her.

Not a proper one anyway.

Had it been long enough since Nick to know this wasn't a rebound situation?

Did it matter whether this was a rebound?

Yes.

No.

Kinda.

Why not just stop trying to control everything?

Just for one night.

Or maybe just the five minutes. And if that worked out, another five after that.

Let fate and random chance take over, and see where she ended up.

Where they ended up.

It couldn't be any worse than where she was now.

She'd deal with tomorrow when it came.

7

Her grip tightened on his arm, and thinking he'd hurt or offended her, his shoulders tensed and his heart kicked into overdrive.

He closely examined her face, and when she closed her eyes, wondered if he'd given her a stroke as well.

That would be embarrassing to report back to Steve. He'd never hear the end of it.

The man who killed his blind date within an hour of meeting her.

She gasped, and her cheeks flushed red, and he had to bite his lip to stop himself putting the back of his hand to her forehead to check her temperature.

Then she opened her eyes and looked up at him.

He sucked in his breath.

He was sure her eyes were green, but looking again, they were more of a dark turquoise.

Deep enough to drown in.

He suppressed a giggle, wondering if he might be about the meet the superhero herself.

Her eyes narrowed slightly as she focused on his lips. There was a new wildness about her, and he was distracted by the idea she might not be a superhero at all.

She might be a supervillain instead.

"Your place," she said, her voice a little huskier than before.

"What?"

"Catch the tram closer to your place."

"Oh," he laughed with distracted nerves, well aware her arm was still tucked in his elbow, and she hadn't released her vice-like grip on his forearm.

"I thought for a minute you meant something else."

She smiled slowly, "maybe I did, but it might be a little too soon for that don't you think?"

Well, no, because:

he was a guy, and

this evening was already so fantastical nothing would surprise him, and

Yes. Please!

"Depends, I can have a meal on the table for you in less than half an hour, and we don't even need to stop off for ingredients on the way."

She stood a little taller, pushing her breasts a little closer towards him, "is that a fact?"

He leaned slightly closer to her, "yes. That *is* a fact."

She took a tiny step towards him, almost touching him, "well then. I dare you to make me dinner."

His briefs felt a little constricting, but he stayed where he was, enjoying the feelings and sensations Norah had aroused.

He cleared his throat, "oh, well, if it's a dare then..."

"Seeing as we've already lied to Mariel once, let's walk down to the next tram stop so they don't see us heading in the wrong direction."

She grinned, and he wondered whether a supervillain might not be more fun than a superhero.

8

As they started walking again, Norah wasn't exactly certain what had gotten into her. Aside from one and a half very tasty serves of alcohol on an empty stomach.

Maybe it was simply that Daniel *saw* her, instead of through her, a sensation she was more than passingly familiar with.

At work, the supermarket, the tram.

The bit of it that perplexed her, was that she generally preferred to be invisible.

More than happy to be ignored by people, especially men.

Certainly the young men at work, (though any kind of non-professional relationship would be inappropriate in so many ways).

And particularly the men her age, who were more interested in women his age.

At a wild guess, he was ten or twenty years younger than her.

God forbid any more.

28

She might even have been married to Nick when Daniel was born.

And that was an appalling possibility.

But.

She *wanted* him, singly and specifically, to *see* her.

And she'd just met him.

He was pretty. And positive. Seemingly untouched by the mess life can be.

Like a firefly - a beautiful light, bright distraction in the darkness. Gone by the morning.

Weird.

And uncomfortable.

Cradle Snatcher. Cougar. Sugar Mummy.

And not technically correct, but peedo.

They paused at the tram stop to wait, and she was quickly chilled by the wind funnelling down the road.

She shivered, and he stepped between her and the wind, shielding her with his body. He took her hands, and after an assessing pause, pushed them into his coat pockets.

"I'd have thought you'd wear something warmer."

She snorted, but didn't move her hands, "no point carrying a coat when you're only going to need it for five minutes."

"I'm guessing then, you live in the inner city and aren't used to long waits for public transport."

She shook her head, mainly to avoid opening her mouth to reveal her teeth chattering, and to warm her cheeks in the heat of his body.

As if he knew what she was up to, he wrapped the front of his coat around her body, dislodging her hands from his pockets in the process.

She squeaked and went rigid.

Then felt him laughing.

"I'm not giving it up for you, but I'm prepared to share."

She was too cold to care about how it might look, and technically she was already on her way to a serial killer/con man's house, so what did it matter if she got snuggly with him in the street to avoid freezing to death in the meantime.

Though they do say you should avoid being taken to a secondary location.

She tucked her hands up under her chin as she turned her head to one side to lean her face against his chest.

She closed her eyes to bask in his spicy warmth and listened to his heart beating.

"Are you right down there?" his voice resonant from that angle.

She nodded, his shirt surprisingly smooth against her cheek.

When the tram arrived, he held out a hand to help her up the steps and gestured for her to precede him into an empty pair of seats.

Another tiny act of unaccustomed civility, and she guessed his mother and grandmother were women to be reckoned with.

It was a nicer explanation than his being a con artist.

Though if he was, she was starting to think he was going to work hard to earn every last one of her cents.

She smiled at the idea of so much effort for so little reward.

He bumped her shoulder with his, "what?"

She grunted.

"What are you smiling about?"

"Nigerian Princes."

"Nigerian Princes?"

"Yes. They must work really hard for the money they scam."

He frowned out the window, "what?"

"You know, finding aliases, finding marks, chatting them up online, phone calls, all that stuff."

"Mmmm. I'd rather find a proper job."

She snorted. "I read somewhere that retired porn stars sometimes find it hard to form close relationships, I wonder if Nigerian Princes are the same."

"I think you're assuming they're independent agents, not working for someone else."

She grunted again, speculating about scamming for a wage instead of yourself.

They got off the tram and started walking. As the cold started sobering her up, she became increasingly nervous about what she'd find when she arrived at his house.

She heard vegetation rustling behind her, then the sound of rain hitting the ground behind them, chasing them up the street.

He grabbed her hand and started running, pulling her behind him.

But the sound grew louder as the rain grew closer and heavier, and not much later, the first cold, wet drops stung her face as they fell.

And suddenly they'd arrived at his house, but soaked through.

He opened a white heritage wire gate and stood back to let her dash down a herringbone-patterned brick path edged with dwarf lavenders.

She stood dripping on the porch, admiring the charming Federation style white weatherboard cottage. And the enormous dormant wisteria growing on wires across the tiny front verandah.

She glanced at his modern, edgy styling as he joined her, then around the overgrown, old-fashioned romantic garden, and rusty steel carport covering a blue car.

Did he still live with his parents?

Or would he call it taking care of his parents?

He wrestled with the door for a moment, before opening it to reveal a worn period interior; high ceilings, white walls, and dark floorboards.

The broken plaster, wattle and daub walls and holes in the ceiling made it obvious he was not with his parents, but renovating an old, and unloved house.

What would the place become, she wondered.

"Hold on a sec'," he said, pushing open the first door on the left and releasing the smell of clean laundry. He flicked a light switch to reveal a room with a neatly made bed, and steel racking containing boxes, power tools, and folded fabrics.

For an instant, she imagined them making love on the bed before blushing and turning away so she couldn't see it or him.

He gathered some things together then led her further down the hall and pushed open the door to a charming old, green bathroom.

Not yet renovated, but probably clean.

Maybe even cleaner than her own.

He put the bundle on a stool just inside the door, with a suit hanger on top.

"Take a shower and get warmed up. I'll be down the other end when you're ready."

He shut the door as he left, and she stood dripping for a minute or two, listening, in case he came back.

It wasn't exactly how she'd imagined getting naked with him, but in the shower might be fun.

She shivered convulsively, then peeled off her wet jacket. Kind of him to consider she might want to hang her suit to dry.

Presumably, he'd be doing the same.

Luckily her skirt was the kind with tapes in the waist, so it went on the hanger, and the hanger on the towel rail.

She dropped the rest of her clothes on the floor before taking a quick shower. Trying unsuccessfully not to imagine the last journey the tablet of soap made before she got to it.

Obviously his clothes were too big for her, but she was too cold not to put them all on, even though she had to roll the waist of his track pants down and the legs up.

It would do.

She might be flirting with the idea of seducing him, but she probably wouldn't.

Most likely couldn't in these clothes.

She rearranged all her clothes on the hanger and left them dripping from the shower rail.

She left her shoes tucked under the stool, picked up her bag, and followed the smell of frying bacon to the back of the house.

In this area at least, the renovation appeared complete.

He'd taken down the walls to open up the space, in a combined kitchen, dining and lounge across the full width of the back of the house.

The kitchen had blond wood cupboards topped with benches made of grey stone, or maybe concrete. Rows of open shelves showcased glass jars of foodstuffs, coloured crockery and copper saucepans.

A plain, angular dining table and chairs in matching wood filled the space between the kitchen island and two square, art deco, steeled framed couches bracketing a coffee table at the lounge end.

Shelves of books and art objects surrounded a wall-hung television.

None of it new though, and she wondered if the furniture was from his family or he'd bought it at an auction or something.

Or it came with the house.

He'd also taken down the ceiling to reveal the rafters, currently decorated with lights and climbing plants. The white walls and dark floorboards were in keeping with the rest of the house.

From the corridor, it made a pleasing collection of right angles against the back wall of glass windows. Too dark to see the garden, but perhaps as old-fashioned and pretty as the front.

The heating kicked in, the sound of air rushing through the vents almost covering the soft music coming from somewhere; rock, but with an orchestral undertone.

So.

He was young, and while he seemed modern, he was only modern in so far as he was daring and decisive; maybe a little adventurous.

He stood barefoot in the kitchen, wet hair closer to brown than blond, dressed in jeans and a loose t-shirt. He was stirring a pot of something that smelled delicious savoury on the enormous stove with a wooden spoon.

"Here you are," he said, putting the spoon down on a plate beside the cooktop and turning to look at her "are you okay?"

She shrugged one shoulder.

He pulled something from his pocket and lobbed it at her, "put these on."

These, were a pair of thick socks, warm from his pocket.

She left her bag on a dining chair, and sat on a black leather lounge, pushing a red and blue plaid blanket aside.

Once she'd pulled the socks on, her feet felt warmer, and so did the rest of her.

Though she was tempted to wrap herself in the blanket too.

By the time she was done, he'd set a mug of steaming tea on the coffee table in front of her.

She wrapped her hands around it to warm them up and took a sip.

Black and a little smoky. Most likely Oolong.

Strange choice for a young man, but one of her favourite teas.

At work, dressed in a suit, she was poised, self-assured and confident. Given she supervised 15 staff, commanding too.

But in Daniel's house, naked under his clothes, she was very conscious of her ageing, saggy body.

And felt uncertain.

Watching his young muscles tense and release as he chopped and stirred. Imagining them clinging to her, she was embarrassed at the thought of him seeing her less than nubile physique.

Embarrassed at the thought she might like him more than he liked her.

And wondered whether men her age felt the same.

Or did they believe their wealth would make up for their lack of fitness and stamina? Were they happy with part-time, cash funded affection?

Could she be happy with $500 dates or did she need more?

Not that she could afford $500 dates - $250 dates? $100 dates?

He smiled over his shoulder at her. "It's not what I planned," he said, "but I hope you enjoy it."

"What?" She blushed, thinking he'd somehow divined her thoughts.

"Soup, I made bacon and corn chowder. It seemed like the right thing for the circumstances."

"Oh," she laughed, more embarrassed now she knew he was saying something innocent.

"Tea okay?"

"Yeah it's fine, I'm just tired."

And as soon as she spoke the lie, she realised it was actually true.

She was tired.

A long, end of month deadline-driven day at work, the stupid birthday party, then god help her, going home with a stranger.

She really should get up and get a cab home.

In a minute or five.

She put her tea down, curled her legs up onto the couch, tucking her feet under the blanket. And laid her head across its back to watch him.

He smiled, "then rest for a moment, there's plenty of time."

She closed her eyes.

9

Even though he'd told her to rest, Daniel was surprised she'd fallen asleep.

He struggled to decide whether it was a good thing or a bad thing?

On the one hand, she was clearly relaxed enough around him to let her guard down.

On the other, was he so boring he'd effectively anaesthetised her?

Dressed in his rolled-up clothes, with her hands curled up under her chin, she looked like a child dressing up in her father's clothing.

Sleeping secure in the knowledge that he was there to protect her from the monsters.

Not a superhero, and not a supervillain.

Just a woman who'd been left alone with a wooden spoon and saucepan lid to protect herself against the monsters.

He opened out the blanket and laid it over her, gently tucking it around her body.

Then turned the soup, music, and main lights off.

He stood in the doorway for an age, trying to decide whether to go to his bed, take the other couch, or maybe sit next to her.

In case she woke up and freaked out.

He put the tv on to catch the late-night news, and without really thinking about it, sat on his favourite couch.

The one she was curled up on.

All bad news as usual, but he'd fallen asleep to it so many times in the past, it was next to no time before he'd fallen asleep as well.

He woke hungover and hungry.

With a warm body snuggled up in his lap.

He panicked and froze for a second, until he realised he was on his couch, in his lounge room, in his house.

Fully clothed, lying under a blanket, with the tv burbling quietly in the background.

He was unbelievably reassured by his clothes, but just to be sure, moved his hand a little, and discovered he was spooning with a woman who was also clothed.

It seemed good evidence the thing he couldn't remember doing, did not, in fact happen.

Though he was pretty sure he hadn't drunk so much he'd forget.

He blinked a couple of times, trying to clear his eyes and brain, and remember who he was with.

Then he tried to get his right arm out from under the blanket, the first step in extricating himself from the situation.

She made a grumbly noise and pulled his hand up and around her body, holding it in both of hers, tucked against the crook of her neck.

Snuggling further down into his groin.

Alarming, but, still fully clothed on the couch. Even if his jeans were becoming a little too tight.

Because it was morning, and she was a woman, even if he couldn't remember who she was at that moment.

Who was warm, and smelled soapy, and real.

He pulled his left arm out from beneath himself, and levered himself into a semi-sit, looking down on her.

Not that he could see much. But there was something familiar about the curve of her neck.

His stomach grumbled, and she kissed his hand and mumbled something.

Did she know who he was, or did she think he was someone else?

Her dead husband maybe?

Norah.

That's it, her name was Norah.

Good, got that sorted.

Feeling embarrassed, he tried to pull his right hand free.

Though why he should feel embarrassed when her husband was dead and nothing untoward had happened was a question for another day.

Except maybe that now he'd got his hand free, but was holding her breast with it.

And she was arching her back and leaning into it.

Her breast was warm and soft, curiously malleable.

Implant free? He couldn't really tell with his clothes in the way.

He couldn't seem to stop himself exploring further.

She did not have rock hard abs. Or Obliques. Or pecs. Her body yielded when he pressed it.

Was this what a "normal" body was like, or was this what happened as you aged?

It was fascinating.

He smoothed his hand lower, and maybe, she kind of moved her body, so he had better access.

She gasped as his fingers pushed beneath the waist of the track pants and he froze.

He couldn't tell if she'd just woken up appalled by what he was doing, and waited for a sign from her telling him what she wanted.

He wasn't sure what he wanted.

He didn't want this to go any further, because there were a hundred conversations that had to happen first.

But he wanted to continue because her body was fascinating, and he wanted to touch, feel, and taste all of it.

She made a needy noise, and in case he'd misunderstood her, he slowly edged his hand further under the pants.

"Are you sure you want this?" his stubble caught in the skin of her neck as he asked.

She arched her body towards his hand, "yes."

And as his hand dropped lower, she arched her back further, "yes," again.

He had next to no idea what he was doing but lightly ran his fingers over her, circling and probing.

She gasped, so he wrapped his left arm around her body, slipping it under the top and massaging her breast while he did it some more.

"Tell me what you want," he breathed in her ear, and she groaned, spreading her legs.

And then, with gasps and shudders, gave his hands unfettered access to her body. She leaned back and braced herself against him, telling him exactly what to do.

And when she came, it was amazing.

That he had done this thing to her, and that she had let him.

The thing was though, it wasn't his name she'd called out.

10

As her breathing evened out, and her brain started up again, Norah turned to give Nick a kiss.

Only it wasn't Nick.

It was some guy she sort of recognised.

She squealed and rolled off the bed.

Only it wasn't a bed, it was a couch, in a room she didn't immediately recognise.

As she backed away from him, he held his hands up. A declaration of innocence she understood, but wasn't reassured. She backed up a little further.

He smiled a little and pointed up the hall.

She scrambled to her feet and made it to the front door before she remembered why she was there.

She turned to look back down the hallway and remembered where the bathroom was. Ducked in and sat on the toilet.

What was his name again?

Sam? Tan? Van?

Dan?

44

Daniel.

Good. That made it easier.

Norah groaned, rubbed her face and scraped her fingers through her hair.

Nice as it was, what the hell had just happened?

And who gave him permission.

Aside from her, because now that she'd thought about it, he'd asked and she'd definitely said yes.

It had been a while, and nice wasn't really a strong enough word for what it was.

She sighed.

Perhaps she wasn't broken after all. Perhaps she just hadn't found the right person until now.

Though that idea didn't necessarily make her feel any better about calling out her dead husband's name while being touched by a living person.

Had it been so long she couldn't tell the difference between the way Nick mapped out her body and someone else did?

After finishing up on the toilet, she washed her hands, splashed cold water on her face, and rinsed her mouth out.

Attempting to make herself wake up and think like the grown-up she was instead of the teenage girl she had been.

Were her clothes dry?

Not quite.

Were they dry enough to wear them anyway and sneak out?

Only if she was desperate.

She hoisted up Daniel's track pants, folded her arms and looked at her suit.

When Nick was transitioning to end of life care, she'd started reading *Fullmetal Alchemist*, because someone left a copy in some waiting room or other.

It had been something diverting, and unlike a book, she didn't need so much concentration she ended up reading the same sentence again and again trying to make sense of it.

Not that it mattered if she didn't take it in anyway, because it was all there in the pictures and at a glance, she got the gist of it.

She still had that first stolen one, and had filled out the set since then.

Fullmetal had become a life vest. Something she'd clung to as she got through the hard times. And relaxed with in the less hard times.

When she'd first seen the suit, the cut of the jacket reminded her of the military uniform. And when she wore it, she drew strength from it, managed to keep her emotions in check and stay focused on doing the things that needed doing.

It had its own kind of alchemy, purifying the pieces of herself she hadn't known were there. Somehow, she'd stood taller and straighter.

Done all that was required and maintained her dignity.

Poised in public, basket case at home when she took it off.

She leaned her forehead on the wall above the towel rail and banged her head against it a couple of times.

What exactly, was she supposed to do now?

The suit wasn't offering any reasonable alternatives.

She turned to look at herself in the mirror.

She looked as old as she felt.

About one hundred.

Basic politeness demanded she return the favour.

But it had been about 99 years since she'd done anything sexual with another person, and about a thousand since she'd tried to seduce anyone.

She snorted.

Did people seduce each other these days, or was it all just hookups now?

Either way, she had no idea how to start that up.

Not sex, not sucking, not anything else.

What do you do when you let an almost total stranger masturbate you the morning after nothing whatsoever happened?

She shivered as she recalled the rasp of his callused fingers across her belly.

Not helping!

A knock on the door made her jump.

"Uh, Norah? Are you okay in there?"

Even though she knew he couldn't see her, she turned her back to the door and hugged herself, "ummm, not really."

"Do you need me to come in and help with something?"

"Er, no. It's not the kind of thing you can help with."

"I see. Well, when you're ready, there's coffee in the kitchen."

"K, thanks. I'll be out in a minute."

Okay.

Two options.

One; put on her Alchemist uniform, run like hell and get as far away as possible as quickly as possible.

They hadn't exchanged numbers or last names, so he couldn't trace her except through Mariel and Steve.

Would he want to? She couldn't say.

Would he contact them?

Probably not; that would be a difficult conversation whichever way you asked it. Anyway, it was more likely they'd contact him first, and he could get her details just like that.

Or would they contact her first to see if she was okay giving out her number?

And what if he did ring her, would she answer?

Would she meet him?

Would she date him?

Would she take him back to her place?

Fuck! She was thinking too far ahead.

Though wasn't the fucking the actual problem?

Option two; give him the five minutes she'd planned to give him the night before.

Before she'd fallen asleep.

Though she'd been more relaxed about those minutes then, than now.

What must he think of her?

She made another face at herself in the mirror, and ran her fingers through her hair, trying to tidy it up.

Then straightened his clothes around her body and opened the door.

She'd give him five minutes to convince her to stay.

11

Daniel smiled a little, backed away from the bathroom door, and walked back to the kitchen. He filled the coffee machine with coffee and fresh water, then set it off.

He almost couldn't believe she'd let him touch her like that.

Whether she really thought he'd been her husband, or it was just the name that came easiest to her lips was another question.

He started humming a catchy tune he couldn't quite remember. And did a little victory dance when it occurred to him it was a pretty good indication she hadn't been in a serious relationship with anyone else in the meantime.

And then he asked himself why he was happy about that, but couldn't give himself a satisfactory answer.

He should find out when her husband died. Could he search the net, or would he have to call Steve?

He scratched his head as he imagined what Steve might say, and decided he didn't want to talk to Steve about her yet.

He still had to work out what to do about her when she left his home.

Assuming he let her leave.

Did she have any plans for the day? It would be nice to take a day off from renovating; where could he take her?

He looked out the window at the wreckage of his back garden.

Wasn't he getting a little ahead of himself? It was just one moment. Five minutes, maybe ten.

Five minutes with no planning or preparation.

It wasn't like she'd chosen him to be the first after, well, you know.

Was it?

He shook his body out to relieve the tension growing across his shoulders, took a few steps over to the bread box and dropped a couple of slices in the toaster. Then shrugged his shoulders and started humming and dancing his way to the pantry for butter, raspberry jam and honey.

Cutlery and crockery from a cupboard in the island.

Bumping hips with it as he squeezed some oranges for juice.

And as the coffee machine beeped its finish, he turned and noticed she was leaning on the corner of the wall, arms folded and legs crossed at the ankle.

Watching him.

He might have blushed a little.

Then grinned at her when he realised she was still wearing his clothes.

As much as he wanted to, he did not whoop when she smiled back.

Though he had the sneaking feeling her smile was more amused tolerance than friendship, or anything deeper.

She didn't look much less rumpled than before, and he wondered whether she was the supervillain or superhero this morning? Probably not well dressed enough for the villain.

Did they share an alter ego or each have their own?

God, now he was giving her a personality disorder.

She shrugged herself off the wall and slinked across the room.

Regardless of who was approaching the kitchen island, she had an edge of steel about her.

Would it hurt when she drew his blood, or would he bleed out so quickly he wouldn't have time to feel it?

A strangely comforting thought.

He dragged his thoughts back from an alternate reality where she wielded a katana with ruthless efficiency to the reality he was standing in.

The one where her suit still hung in his bathroom.

"Let me guess," he said, "black with none?"

She snorted, and pulled a stool a little out from the island and climbed onto it, "close, black with one."

He poured coffee, added sugar, gave it a stir and pushed it across the bench at her.

She picked it up and held it in both hands as she closed her eyes to inhale its smoky perfume. As if it was the finest wine.

"Not a morning person then?" he asked as he made his own.

She opened one eye, lifted one side of her lips in a smile, and grunted.

The toast popped, and he juggled it to the plate in front of her before dropping more into the toaster. She put a slice onto the other plate and slid it back towards him before smearing butter and honey on hers.

He winced as she dipped the butter knife in the honey jar, and again as she dropped the dirty knife on his new, clean bench, but didn't say anything about it.

Daniel leaned one hip against his side of the island as he ate.

She was doing a good job of pretending to be at ease, but she perched on the edge of the stool, and her body was tense.

He had the idea if he got too close she'd freak out, abandon her clothes and be gone before he could blink.

And freak out if he suggested they continue where they'd left off earlier.

Not exactly sure what he could do without freaking her out.

Making breakfast was a good way to give her a little space while keeping her there a little longer. He could keep toast and coffee coming for as long as it took. But how long did he have to come up with something else to do?

The fact of Winter made it a bit difficult.

Drive to the country for lunch, or some coffee?

His phone started ringing, and he took it from his pocket.

"Steve," he said, glancing at her and dropping the phone on the island.

"You don't want to answer that?"

He snorted, "and what exactly do you think is going to be the first question he asks?"

"Ah," she blushed quite dark.

"Has Mariel tried you?"

"Don't know, I always leave my phone on silent." She took a bite of toast.

"What? Why?"

"I need to focus at work, and all that ringing and pinging disrupts my concentration."

Daniel couldn't get his head around the idea, "aren't you worried you'll miss something important?"

She shrugged one shoulder, "my message tells people I turn the phone off when I'm working and they should leave a message."

"And if they don't?"

She shrugged, "can't be important then, can it?"

"Are you going to check now?"

"Why would I?"

Daniel looked at her, then picked up his phone, waved it at her, and put it down again.

She shook her head, "isn't it a little early for that?" she twisted her wrist to look at her watch, "oh. Perhaps not."

He picked his phone back up to check the time, just as a text came in, "you probably should check; Mariel's worried about you. You want me to tell them you're okay?"

"Oh, for god's sake, it's not like they're my parents!"

She slid from the stool, skating a little as his socks hit the floor, and pulled her phone from her bag.

"27 missed calls. First one 8:02. She didn't waste any time, did she?"

Daniel laughed, "What story do you want to tell them?"

She frowned at him, "you should've woken me up so I could go home, and we could've avoided all this."

The toast popped, so he put his phone down again, slid a slice onto her plate and one on his, then refilled the toaster and dropped the toast.

"More coffee while you're storming there?"

Norah put her phone on the counter and climbed back onto the stool. "It's all right for you, you're not the one who's going to get the responsibility lecture."

"Responsibility lecture?"

She frowned at him, "something along the lines of being old enough and wise enough not to go home with strangers."

"Ah," he refilled the coffee maker with fresh water and coffee and turned it on too. "But didn't you tell her something came up? I'd have thought she'd be more concerned about that."

"Fuck!" She texted furiously, "I'm not saying anything about you, just that I'm fine."

"Then I won't say anything at all."

She smiled impishly up at him, "thanks."

"Don't thank me, they'll figure it out for themselves."

"Then I shall neither confirm nor deny any allegations they make."

He snorted.

Things were looking up; she might not confirm (though it was way too soon for that), but at least she would not deny.

She buttered her second slice of toast, then hovered her knife for a moment before dipping it in the jam.

Much as the cross-contamination annoyed him, he didn't say anything. It wasn't the end of the world, it was just jam. He had a spare in the pantry anyway, he would just throw that one out.

Next time, he'd put a teaspoon in the pot, and hopefully, she'd take the hint.

"So if we're all fine," he said, "seeing as we missed dinner last night, would you like to do something together today?"

12

Norah looked up at him mid-chew.

She could feel her mother's look of disgust and mild contempt sliding across her face.

It wasn't exactly the way she felt, though she did feel uncomfortable.

He was like a puppy, all hopeful expectation. She could almost see his tail wagging in anticipation.

He couldn't be much more than half her age, and those 20-odd years bothered her a great deal more over breakfast than it had the night before.

It wasn't exactly what he'd asked, but she had the feeling he was suggesting a date, not a carpool to the supermarket.

Though maybe a carpool to a farmer's market might not be a bad thing.

She put a hand up to run through her white hair and easily imagined kindly stallholders telling him he was a good boy for taking his mother shopping.

She shuddered a little, maybe they'd think she was his grandmother.

Norah realised she was staring at him, looked down at her plate and swallowed the toast.

Accidentally taking a breath at the same time and starting to cough as she inhaled some crumbs.

Then tried to drink some coffee to clear it up but that just made her cough it up and spit it down the front of herself.

And his nice clean hoodie.

So much for mature, confident and assured woman.

She was doing that teenager thing again.

Keep that up, and those stall holders'd be thinking she was demented as well.

Daniel threw a tea towel at her and sprinted around the island to thump her back.

She burped, then shoved the breakfast things out of her way and lay her head on the bench.

Bang slap into a small puddle of jam she'd obviously left there when she dropped the knife.

She groaned.

Was there anything more she could do to embarrass herself even further?

Before this precocious child?

Aside from maybe bang her head a few times on the bench.

As if banging it on the bathroom wall hadn't been enough already.

She'd be concussed before too long.

"Um. Are you okay Norah?"

His face was so close she nearly head-butted him as she raised her head to look at him, "I have jam on my face, don't I?"

He cradled her cheek with his left hand, wiped a smear off with his thumb, then licked it, "not any more."

She felt her breasts swell as she remembered him swiping her nipple with a thumb earlier.

She looked at the tiny bead of jam he'd left on his upper lip, and wondered what would happen if she licked it off.

He was looking at her as if she was a bomb about to go off, but didn't move away as she leaned closer.

And closer.

Close enough to smell the jam on his breath.

And still, he didn't move.

Was he curious too?

She pressed her lips to his, her tongue darting out to lick it off.

As she drew back, he groaned deep within his throat, grabbed her shoulders and pulled her back to him, kissing her deeply.

Sliding his arms around her body, and stepping between her legs.

She scooted forward, closer to the edge of the stool, intoxicated by the warm scent of his body.

The strength of his arms, and as his hands slipped under the back of the hoodie, the roughness of those callouses again.

It was like sliding beneath a hot bubble bath.

Only less wet.

Well, maybe only slightly less wet.

And if she didn't get her shit together, she was going to melt into a puddle at his feet and be sucked inside his body, never to be seen again.

Okay, that was an exaggeration, but she had to stop this thing before it went too far.

Reluctantly, she leaned away from him, and reluctantly he let her go.

"I'm sorry," she said, "I can't do this."

"Do what?"

"This," she waved a hand between the two of them, "this thing. Whatever it is."

"Is it to soon?"

"Too soon? What?"

It dawned on her he meant Nick. It wasn't Nick, but he made a convenient excuse, "yes. I'm sorry. I think I'd better leave."

It was too hard to explain he was too young.

He was a beautiful bouncing boy, and she was old and saggy. Worn out and used up.

And anyway, she'd already married THE one.

There could only be one, that's why Nick was the one.

And Daniel wasn't.

To have more than one "One" is just greedy.

She'd had her time, now she had to leave something for the women who came after her.

She slid off the stool, slip slided across the floor to grab her bag and head towards the bathroom.

She threw on her clothes and left without saying goodbye

Daniel heard the door close and wondered if he should chase her.

Didn't women want you to chase them?

Or was that the kind of thing that got you arrested as a stalker?

But if she wasn't over her husband, he wasn't going to be the one to force her.

There were plenty of other fish in the sea.

So he'd been told.

Though he didn't think he wanted some other fish.

For the moment.

He left the wreckage of breakfast on the bench, carried his coffee over to the window, and stood looking out into the garden.

It really was a mess, he should've been more careful about disposing of the timber offcuts, and pouring out the leftover paint and plaster.

Why hadn't he taken more care with what had once been a charming garden?

Probably because the highly scented flowers felt like an insult to his manliness or some other kind of stupidity.

He sipped his coffee and wondered if relaxing in the garden in Spring would smell like Norah was sitting right next to him.

He'd probably never find out. He'd probably never see her again and would have forgotten her scent by then.

Only now that he was looking, with the idea of sharing in mind, he could see what the finished garden would be like.

Open out the glass doors onto a flat courtyard; it would be a pleasant place to sit looking up at the garden. Add a pergola for grapes or wisteria to shade the back of the house. A veggie patch up the back, some planters for herbs on the courtyard.

And just like that, he had a plan.

If he levelled out the courtyard first, he'd have a good size working space. Add some large bins there'd be somewhere to dump the renovation waste.

And a couple of benches, somewhere to relax with a beer or a cuppa in the meantime.

And being a bit frustrated and feeling a bit aggressive made this the perfect opportunity to make a start.

He challenged himself to take a ute load of rubbish to the tip that day.

But first, he drew a rough plan so he wouldn't forget what he was thinking.

Leaving his mug on the bench, he grabbed a couple of grubby bins from the bedroom he was using as a workroom and went outside to get started.

14

Norah opened her apartment door.

The smell of stagnant, dead air, over-full rubbish bin, and burnt toast rolled out to meet her as she pushed the door open.

Compared to the smells of fried onions and garlic, curry, damp clothes and staleness she'd walked passed to get to her door.

She'd taken the tiny apartment because it was cheap, modern and new.

No previous tenants to leave their energy behind.

But she didn't really need them. The people who lived either side, as well as up and down had plenty of energy to make up for that.

She'd sold the home she'd shared with Nick, and all their furniture with it to pay for his mounting medical expenses. By that time he was in respite care, and all she'd wanted was somewhere small and clean to nap between shifts by his bedside.

Oh, and vacant, because she'd left it too long and had nowhere else to go when the house settled and she had to move out.

She'd just thrown everything into boxes, and her friends had moved it all for her while she sat vigil. And got her a futon mattress to tide her over.

A couple of days later, he was gone.

And a few more later, she discovered the apartment building housed a lot of holiday rentals and therefore wasn't the best place to live permanently.

But by then she was locked into a rolling 12-month lease, and not organised enough to break it as the years rolled by.

She kicked her shoes off in the entry and left them lying haphazardly where they fell.

Her apartment was a rectangle. Kitchen and living on the front street side, bedroom, bathroom come laundry and toilet on the internal corridor side. Not always the best arrangement for sleeping, but better than the street.

For some reason, she walked down the hall to the living area instead of cutting through the bathroom to the bedroom.

And it hit her that the space was still almost completely filled with unopened boxes.

Not that she didn't know they were there, but having just come from Daniel's neat, open space, it was like walking into a wall of brown cardboard.

Almost as if half the apartment didn't exist at all.

What was left of it was dark and gloomy.

Would it be more appealing if the boxes weren't there?

She changed into leggings and one of Nick's old t-shirts, dropping her clothes on her bedroom floor as she undressed.

And shoved her feet into the stinky old ugg boots that really needed replacing. But as they were the last gift he'd bought her, she didn't want to let them go.

No matter how bad they got. And they were so bad they almost walked on their own.

She started to feel like the walls were closing in on her, as if all the oxygen had been used up. She had to get a window open, but the boxes were in the way.

Grabbing the closest box, she tried to wrestle it out of the way, but it was too heavy.

She tried to tear it open, but the tape was still well stuck down, and she needed a blade to slice it open.

In the kitchen, she noticed she didn't have more than one of anything. And again, she compared it to Daniel's well-stocked room.

Renovating or not, he was clearly ready to prepare actual food for himself and others, without notice.

She just made instant noodles and ate them out of the container.

When was the last time she'd cooked for herself, let alone anyone else?

Wasn't that supposed to be what blokes did while women cooked themselves real food?

She laughed derisively at herself. No one looking at her outside this apartment could possibly imagine she lived like this.

At least the fridge was well stocked with beer, so she helped herself and took it with the knife back to the living room.

The box was full of rubbish.

Not literally rubbish, but nothing she wanted to keep. Some of it could go to charity, but most of it was stuffed into her last garbage bag.

She took it down to the bin enclosure, stopping at the small street-level supermarket on the way back for supplies.

A couple of boxes later, she found a penknife and retired her kitchen knife to the sink.

Then took her rubbish down to the bin.

And after coming back in, rearranged the boxes to open some windows to let some light and air in.

Not that it made much difference because the evening was drawing in.

But she felt lighter and freer.

Slightly more cheerful.

As if something in the universe had changed, though she couldn't say what.

She made some instant noodles and ate them as she stood in the window, watching the lights in the apartment building across the road come on and go off.

Like a randomised screen saver.

She wanted to do more but thought she'd watch the news and see what had happened in the world during the day.

Except her phone wasn't in its usual spot on the kitchen bench, or on the floor by her bed, or in her bag.

And then she remembered, she'd left it in Daniel's kitchen when she'd fled his house.

She couldn't ring him, because she didn't have his number.

She couldn't ring Mariel, because her number was only in the phone. The phone she'd left in Daniel's house.

And in any case, the payphone in the building foyer was missing a handset, and she had no idea where the next closest one was.

It seemed the only thing to do, was cross her fingers he'd be home, and go get it.

15

When the doorbell rang, Daniel was naked, on his way to the bathroom to clean up. He was tired, and a bit sore, but satisfied with his progress clearing a space for the courtyard to come.

And seeing as he didn't have room for a bath in the bathroom, he was now thinking maybe a hot tub would be a good addition to the courtyard

He wasn't expecting anyone and was tempted to ignore the door.

But the bell rang a couple of times more, suggesting urgency, so he dragged on his filthy work clothes back on, leaving his shirt hanging open, and answered.

He didn't recognise what he thought was an ordinary girl, dressed in a long coat, jeans, sneakers, and a shirt that buttoned diagonally across her chest.

Until she stepped into the light.

"Norah."

"Um, hi. Did I leave my phone here when I left?"

"Yeah, but I'm getting ready to head out," he lied, "you should have called."

She half-smiled, and he remembered, "your phone's on silent."

She nodded.

He still couldn't get his head around her not checking her phone.

"Wait here, I'll get it for you," he said, and shut the door in her face.

The afternoon digging in the garden had been exhausting, but hadn't really soothed his anger towards her.

Made it stronger if anything.

Much as he thought he wanted Norah, he'd been chased more than once by girls he didn't want, and he didn't plan to embarrass himself by his persistence.

And was too proud to beg her anyway.

If she changed her mind, she'd have to come crawling back and work really hard to convince him.

As he walked down the hallway, he debated with himself about making her wait out in the cold and then hated himself for thinking of doing that to anyone mid-winter, let alone her. So, he wasted no time grabbing her phone and taking it back.

When he opened the door, her back was toward him, her head looking down to the side. She hadn't heard the door open, so he had a moment to study her.

With her hands shoved in the pockets of her large coat, she was unremarkable.

Not super anything.

Nothing whatsoever about her that would make him give her a second glance.

In fact, she seemed limp. Forlorn even. Maybe super sad.

He felt guilty.

She had every right to feel uncertain - she'd lost her husband.

No one could just get over than and move on.

If only he knew what she was afraid of, he could counter her fears.

He cleared his throat, and she spun around, her coat flaring like a cape.

And he realised after her hasty exit, it must have cost her a great deal to come back.

Or if you looked at it that way, come crawling back.

"Ah, did you want to come in?"

She rocked on her heels, "no. No, that's fine. You said you're just about to head out. I'll just take my phone and go."

She held out her hand, but he held her phone back against his chest.

"If you don't mind waiting, I could drop you somewhere on the way."

She was staring at his chest, so he leaned on the door frame, dropping his arm and tensing his muscles a little.

Letting his shirt fall open a little further.

This time he saw her green eyes darken to turquoise, and her pupils dilate and knew she found him physically attractive.

Not that it was a battle, but if it was, he'd half won.

She licked her lips, and when she glanced at his crotch before looking up and into his eyes, leaning on the door frame became the hardest thing he'd ever done.

He took a step back to hold the door open for her.

Norah hesitated, looked up at him, but whatever she saw convinced her.

She stepped over the threshold and walked towards the back of the house.

When he caught up, she was staring up at his kitchen shelves.

He glanced up at them, wondering if she'd seen a spider or a mouse, but they looked fine.

"Would you like some tea?"

"What? Oh, no. No, I'm fine. You go get ready."

"It's no trouble."

She snorted, "okay fine, I'll have tea."

He grinned, and for a second everything was perfect.

Then she abruptly turned away.

He left her phone on the island, turned to fill the kettle and turned it on.

Was it possible she felt she was being disloyal to her husband?

He took a couple of mugs down and added some leaf tea to a pot.

How long was long enough to mourn?

Yesterday, he'd got the idea she was ready to move on, but what if she'd discovered she wasn't?

What if she just needed a friend?

Someone tall enough to change the light globes, and computer literate enough to troubleshoot her laptop?

He could do that.

It wasn't like he was ready to give her forever anyway.

Yesterday his plan was only to give her a couple of hours.

Maybe having sex was too complicated.

Maybe taking up space inside her head would be better than taking up space inside her body.

A chick, who was a friend, who he could test chat up lines and stuff on.

Get a more experienced opinion about what girls want.

He turned around to give her the tea, saw her phone had disappeared into a pocket, and she was smiling into the book she was reading.

"Tea's made," he said. "I'll just take a quick shower, make yourself at home."

She turned, book in hand, and extended her smile to him, before turning back to the book.

He took the quickest shower possible and was back within five minutes.

Dressed in jeans and his lucky blue jumper.

She didn't seem to have moved.

"Team Ed or Al?" she asked.

"You know *Fullmetal Alchemist*?"

"Love it!"

"How did you... Never mind. Al all the way," he replied.

"Ah, crazy cat boy eh?"

He snorted, "someone else's cat turns up out there now and again to sunbathe in my garden. You?"

"Ed."

"Because you're short?"

"I am not short!" she laughed. "Because he wears black! Anyway, I'd've thought Roy Mustang might be more your style?"

"Because I'm hot?"

She laughed, shaking her head, "you are, but that's not the reason."

He did a little dance, and sang along, "you think I'm ho-ot, you think I'm ho-ot, you think I'm ho-ot."

"Yeah, but you're also a snappy dresser, a bit of a flirt, and possibly fiendishly clever."

He scratched his chin as he walked across to her, "well, definitely a snappy dresser *and* fiendishly clever. Bit of a Flirt? Hmmm. Yeah, okay, I'm a bit of a flirt too. But I promise I'm not planning to take over the military.

"Any more intel I can fill you in on?"

"All right then Colonel, *Star Wars* or *Star Trek*?"

He pretended to think, "*Star Wars*."

"No. Way."

"No, I'm kidding, *Babylon 5* all the way."

"Classic. Nice. I'd like to live in *Star Trek*, but I think the reality would be more like *Babylon 5*."

"Then who's your favourite Captain?"

"Lorca."

"Oh, interesting choice, very controversial."

Norah raised an eyebrow.

"Archer. Mine's Jonathan Archer."

"I'll pay that," she said, and put the book back where she'd found it.

Daniel was glad. After the jam incident that morning, he'd been afraid she'd just shove it back anywhere.

"You've got your phone, so shall I take you home now?"

"Sure. I'm sorry I'd forgotten you had a date."

Not sure why, but he really wanted her to know his imaginary appointment wasn't with a girl.

He gestured towards the front of the house, "it's not a date, just meeting friends."

She walked out the door and waited on the porch while he locked it.

He gestured at the car. As she walked toward it, he pushed the button on his key ring, and the locks disengaged. He opened the door for her then walked around to the driver's side.

Should he have shut the door for her?

No, she was fiddling with her coat, trying to get comfortable, so he pushed the button to turn the seat warmers on.

"Address?"

She laughed, "of course you need to know where to go, and gave him the address."

He backed out the drive, and they were on their way.

She blew on her hands and rubbed them together.

"It won't be long until the heat kicks in. You could sit on your hands in the meantime, the seat warmers are much quicker."

She looked at him, then shrugged and pushed her hands underneath her, "ah, that's lovely."

"Best thing in winter."

"I can tell. Beats hanging around for a tram I bet."

"I usually take the tram to work, it's a tiny bit quicker, plus I don't have to pay for parking."

"What do you do?"

"I'm a Project Manager at a construction company."

She snorted, "that's funny, I'm a Project Manager in the Public Service."

"Really? That *is* funny. What are you working on at the moment?"

"Can't tell you, it's confidential at the moment."

"And you'd have to kill me?"

"I thought we'd already established you're the serial killer in this relationship."

He snorted, "how does the confidentiality aspect work.

"Just adds another layer of Risk Management."

"I can imagine."

"Let's not talk about work," she said, and pushed the button to turn the radio on. The car filled with the soft sounds of Norah Jones.

"I love this song," she said and started humming along.

He glanced at "his" Norah, who seemed more relaxed than he'd expected.

Her apartment was near the building he parked in when he drove to work, so he pulled in there.

"I'll walk you to your apartment," he said.

"Thanks, but I don't want to interrupt your plans. I'll be fine to walk home from here."

"Are you serious, do you know what kind of area you live in?"

"You know I do, but this kind of area is usually safe for the people who live in them."

"I don't care. I'd never hear the end of it if you were attacked on your way home."

"Mariel's not that bad."

"You don't get it, it's my version of the responsibility lecture."

"How does yours go?"

"Along the lines of making sure you don't get hurt, killed or kidnapped on your way home."

"Tedious, wouldn't you rather skip that.

"I would, that's why I'm walking you. Don't forget that woman who was dragged into a side street and assaulted last month."

"Okay fine."

He led the way out of the parking structure. "Do you know you say "fine" a lot?"

"Do I?"

"Yes."

"I hadn't noticed."

"Are you really fine, or is it something you say to deflect people?"

"I'm fine-ish. I guess I got used to saying it while Nick was... sick, to stop people asking questions."

He wondered if she was thinking of the last time she said her husband's name.

He pretended not to notice.

"Like when people ask how you are, and you say good."

"Yes, because you just don't want to get into it."

"I see."

"And some people think you're not sad enough, so they try to make you display what they think is a more appropriate level of emotion."

"That must be annoying."

"It is. And a little hurtful. Not all of us have the luxury of falling to pieces. Some of us have no choice but to keep going. Keep pushing the feelings so deep down we can't feel them."

"Must be hard."

"Yeah. Sometimes I think I numbed them all down for so long, I can't feel at all."

She stopped, "we're here, you can go now."

He looked up at the ugly building, it didn't look much safer than the street.

"I said I'd see you to your door. This is not your door."

"It's a security door - once I'm inside, no one can get to me."

"Except anyone who's already loose in there."

"I told you, I'm fine."

He crossed his arms and rocked on his heels.

She made a face, and he laughed as she swiped her key over the reader.

They took the elevator and walked down a corridor.

"This is me," she said, pausing halfway down.

He gestured at the door; she made a frustrated noise, opened it and turned to face him.

"Thanks for seeing me home," she said, with a bob that may or may not have been a curtsey.

"No problem. Don't forget to ring Mariel."

She made a face, "yes. I suppose I should do that. She'll want to know what happened."

"Tell her you had such a great time, you had to see me again."

Norah blushed, "I suppose I did, Colonel."

He pointed a thumb over his shoulder in the direction of the lift well, "I got you home, I guess I should go..."

She looked at him for a few seconds, reading him again, "or you could come in."

Daniel stepped through the doorway before she could change her mind.

16

As soon as Norah said the words, she started calling herself names and asking what the hell she thought she was thinking.

For one thing, the place was a pigsty, and for another, the only thing she had more than one of was beer.

And packets of instant noodles.

As long as he didn't open any cupboards, or the drudge, or need to go to the bathroom, she could probably bluff her way through it.

She lengthened her stride and caught up with him just as he reached the end of the hallway and looked into the lamp-lit living room.

He turned to look at her, "nice place you have here Fullmetal. Are you just moving in?"

Norah screwed up her face, "not exactly."

"Ah. Moving out then. Good job too."

She looked around, seeing the room through his eyes, and it was completely devoid of charm.

Not just the room, but the entire apartment.

She couldn't believe she'd lived there so long and hadn't noticed.

"Not exactly that, either."

Daniel looked around and made a helpless gesture.

"I just haven't unpacked yet."

"You haven't unpacked? How long have you been here?"

Norah's eyes burned with the threat of tears as she looked at her watch. "I don't know, about five years."

Daniel's jaw dropped, and his eyes widened, "you've lived in this hell hole for five years?"

She half sobbed half snorted, "time flies when you're having fun."

"Are you having fun?"

She refused to meet his eyes, "no. Not really."

He made another helpless gesture, "then how..."

"I had to sell the house to pay the bills, and Nick was in palliative care, and I just threw everything into boxes and took the first place I found."

She closed her eyes, and screwed her face up, but couldn't stop the tears leaking through.

"And I was never here, and then he died, and I just couldn't face opening the boxes."

She took a deep breath, "there were arrangements to make, and I just had to just keep things moving along, and there never seemed to be enough time, and after a while, I just didn't see them anymore, and here we are."

She looked around the room again and rubbed her face as if that would make everything disappear, "this wasn't how it was supposed to be."

Embarrassed, she turned away and bent over as if she'd been punched in the guts, gasping as she tried to catch her breath, to stop crying, to stop being so pathetic.

"I don't know how you coped."

She laughed, sort of, and wiped her nose on her sleeve.

"First, who says I'm coping, and second, who says I have a choice. I just do what needs to be done."

"But didn't you take any time off?"

She took a deep breath, and let her proud Fullmetal spirit take over.

"Not that it's any of your business, but I'd already used up all my leave and was taking unpaid leave. After the funeral, I just had to suck it up and get on with it."

"So you've never stopped to feel the pain, to reconcile with it?"

She stiffened and whirled to face him, "No. But what would you know? And why would you care?"

He took a step towards her and pulled her into a hug, holding her tightly. Almost too tightly.

She struggled initially, wanting to bust out of his arms, and get the hell away from him.

And every other fucked up thing in her life.

Which was, in fact, her whole life.

But he held her tightly.

And pressed against his warm body, with nowhere to move, there was no escaping from him or her life.

As he continued to hold her, Fullmetal drained away and some of her tension dissipated. Not exactly relaxed, but not as tightly wound as before the hug.

A little calmer, a little reassured.

She remembered the Squeeze Machine.

The thing that woman designed, based on on the thing that keeps cows calm.

What was that woman's name?

Temperance something?

Temple Grandin.

Dr Temple Grandin.

Was this the kind of thing she was talking about?

What did they call it?

Deep touch.

Maybe she needed a deep touch machine.

Daniel said something. She could feel his chest resonating, but had to lean back and away from him to hear.

"What?"

"How long were you married?"

"Nineteen years, eleven months, three weeks and three days.

"Not that I was counting."

His grip didn't loosen as he slowly patted her back with one hand.

"You poor thing, no wonder."

She stiffened, "I am not a poor thing. And no wonder what?"

"So hard to get so close to twenty years, and lose everything."

Norah's legs gave way as the enormity of it hit her, and she dropped out of the circle of his arms.

In an instant, he crouched down and pulled her to him again."

"I didn't know what to do, because there was nothing I could do. Except pretend I didn't know he was going to die, to give him some peace, let him think everything was okay.

"All I wanted was five more minutes with him, but all our minutes were all used up.

"And now I'm alone, and I don't know how to be alone, and I don't know how to be without him, but I don't know how to be with anyone else."

"And why would you?

"I bet you've known him your whole life, and there isn't a single thought you can have that isn't in some way connected back to him.

"Of *course* you're not fine."

It was as if, for the first time in her life, someone understood.

And someone cared.

And after all that time, something inside her broke, and she couldn't keep it all inside anymore.

She couldn't breathe.

She couldn't stop crying.

Her cheeks hurt from squeezing her eyes shut to try stopping the tears from coming out.

And her throat burned as the sobs forced their way out.

She could hear herself making loud, ugly noises, and her chest hurt so much with the size and depth of her convulsions she had to hold her fist against to try and hold it still.

She was kneeling on something sharp, and it hurt, but she couldn't get her shit together enough to move it or herself out of the circle of his arms.

After about forever, she just wore out and slumped in his arms.

He was stroking her back, crooning, some nonsense she couldn't get a grip on.

"You're going to be fine."

"Will I?" she asked, "will I really?"

"Yes."

She didn't believe him, but she had to ask.

"Promise?"

"Promise."

She twisted around in his arms until she was half sitting on his lap.

"Then who's your favourite Doctor?"

She felt his body shake as he laughed. "You're feeling a little better then?"

"I have a headache."

"I'm not surprised," he eased her off his lap, "I'll get you some water."

She could hear him opening and closing cupboards in the kitchen.

And remembered she couldn't let him open the fridge.

"Not the fridge," she shouted as she scrambled to her feet and overbalanced into the wall.

Too late to stop it, she heard the fridge open, and after a moment, just as she careened around the corner, "is there some reason you don't have any proper food in your house?"

She laughed.

And kept laughing.

And tripped over her feet and laughed some more, still laughing as he caught her before she fell.

Which made her laugh even more until she was laughing uncontrollably hard and struggling to breathe with as much difficulty as when she'd been crying.

Clutching her side as she got a stitch, and laughing at that as well.

Expecting him to run out the door because she was mental and surprised when he wrapped his arms tightly around her again.

Because maybe he knew about the Squeeze Machine too.

If she couldn't get her shit together anytime soon, she'd never find out.

She hiccupped. And shortly after that, another one.

Daniel kept one arm around her, as he rinsed and filled the empty mug in the sink with water from the tap.

"Try to drink out of the wrong side," he said.

A seemingly insurmountable challenge, and by the time she got herself a sip of water, the hiccups were gone.

She became aware of the size of him taking up room in her tiny apartment. The heat of his arm, still clutching her waist and the solidity of his body behind her.

Something to lean on.

But for how long?

She took a deep breath and held it for a count of ten heart-beats before letting it go.

Then drank the rest of the water and leaned over to shove the mug on the bench before curling back onto his chest, within the safety of his arms.

God knew when he was going to get bored of holding her, so she had to take advantage of it while she could.

He'd probably leave as soon as he did get bored, probably set a land speed record on his way out.

After all, he had a thing to go to.

Oh Fuck.

Should she remind him?

Yes.

She should.

But she wasn't going to.

Just meeting friends, he'd said. As if it was unimportant.

Anyway, he'd walked through the door of his own volition, so he was fair game to keep for a while.

Daniel wrapped his other arm back around her and gave her The Squeeze again.

Shrouded in the comforting, clean smell of his soap and laundry detergent, she thought about how fresh it made him seem.

And how stale and jaded she felt by comparison.

Was it because she was getting old, or because the last few years had been an endurance event, and she hadn't gone through a cool-down phase?

Daniel's body was hard and strong, not soft and frail like Nick's had become.

And that was a tragedy. The memory of the lively young man she'd fallen in love with was eclipsed by the memory of the one who died.

The length and extent of his incapacity had made her feel guilty for living.

Guilty for wanting to forget him and move on.

Angry for giving up so much of herself she was an empty husk no one would want.

With her cheek pressed against Daniel's chest, she listened to the slow, steady rhythm of his heart.

How had that nurse described it?

The thrill, the feel of the blood moving in the veins.

Like a drum.

Or in his chest, like a song.

Like his heart was singing her a song.

A siren song.

And she didn't really care, she was already shipwrecked, and life couldn't get any worse.

He had a pulse, and technically, so did she.

Had she buried herself inside this place, or was she in a trap sucking the life out of her?

She certainly felt heavy and lethargic.

And hot.

And something else, hard and hot and strong, against her belly.

Not felt one of those for a while.

Was he aroused?

By her?

She lightly rubbed her abdomen across it as she swapped her weight from one leg to the other, and it leapt against her.

And reminded her of the way he'd touched her that morning.

Her nipples puckered in response, and she felt herself tingling and expanding to accommodate him.

Should she go for it?

If she wanted to let go of the past and move on, there had to be a first.

The second would be easier.

And the third even easier than that.

And he seemed willing.

At least his body did.

And it was dark, so he wouldn't see the wreck she'd become.

Better hope he'd come prepared, so to speak, because she wasn't.

17

Daniel didn't want to want sex with her after her turbulent release of emotion. But holding her close, and smelling her hair was making it difficult not to.

She'd called out his protective streak, and he wanted to be a bit macho for her. And not to feel like he'd taken advantage of her vulnerability.

He tried to think about how awful it must be to lose your other half after such a long time, and how twenty years later, he'd be part of your DNA.

The food you ate, the books you read, the tv shows you watched.

The jokes you told, your sense of humour.

How you'd come home from work to find her cooking you a meal, and the first face you saw in the morning would be hers. And how you'd see her naked so often, you'd hardly blink.

He felt himself start to go hard.

Already he was twisting it to imagine what it would be like to be her husband.

Stepping into a dead man's shoes.

What would it be like to always know there was someone else in her heart.

Ripped away by tragic circumstances as he was, his memory would never tarnish.

Would you always be a little jealous of the man who got there first?

Would she always compare you to him?

Would you always come last?

He felt her move against him, though he couldn't tell whether it was deliberate or not.

Until, after a short pause, she did it again.

And again.

He slid his arms down her back and held her hips, cupping his fingers around her bottom. Partly to stop her moving, and partly to enjoy the feel.

She reached up and wriggled a little as she shrugged her coat off her shoulders.

He gasped, and she smiled a small, seductive smile.

She started unbuttoning her shirt.

"Wait," he said, seizing her hands, holding them against his chest, letting her coat fall to the floor.

She didn't step back, but remained pressed against him.

Head to one side looking quizzically at him.

He struggled to find the right words to say, "what are you doing?"

"Taking my clothes off."

"Why?"

"Didn't your parents tell you about the birds and the bees?"

"Are you sure?"

"We have unfinished business you and I."

"But...," he raised one shoulder, "you won't regret it?"

"One way or another, it's going to get in the way of what comes next for both of us. Once we've had sex, it'll clear the air, and we can decide what to do."

"But, what if one of us wants it more than the other?"

She frowned, "you mean the sex?"

"No, after. Relationships."

"That's true of any relationship. They're always uneven. And some last longer than others."

How had she not stepped back?

How was she still pressed up hard against him?

"But what about your husband?"

"Well, I'm pretty sure he's not in a position to join in."

"No! I mean... You know?"

She raised an eyebrow.

"How you feel about him."

"Oh, I see.

"Would it make you feel better to call this an experiment, or a one night stand?"

He dropped his hands, taking hers with them.

"Daniel," she rubbed against his belly again, "if you don't think you can have sex with me, just say so."

"No, it's not that—"

"Then if you don't make a move quickly, I'll be shooing you out of here, and taking care of business myself."

He leaned forward and kissed her, lightly on the lips.

She tried to pull her hands free, but he waited for a moment before letting them go.

She slid her cool, soft hands under his jumper, pushing them higher up his abdomen, and arched her pelvis against his.

He undid her top button and kissed her chest before undoing the next and kissing her again.

Revealing a bra bigger, lacier, and more colourful than any he'd seen before.

For a moment, he was distracted, tracing the floral pattern with the tip of one finger, making her sigh.

Had she worn it just for him?

He slid the shirt off her shoulders, brushed it down her arms, and let it fall to the floor.

She took his hand and led him into her bedroom, which was terrifyingly like a student squat with a mattress on the floor.

And she'd been living like this for five years? He tried not to think about what her marital bed was like.

She sat on the edge of the mattress, and as his eyes adjusted to the dim light, he could see it was a futon on a low platform.

He was somewhat reassured, maybe she preferred it because she wasn't tall.

But she'd probably bought it in a hurry, and it hurt his heart to think of her living in a place like this.

He resolved to give her the kind of experience that would set her confidently onto a new path.

Whether it led towards him, or someone else.

Because she was right, after what happened that morning, they couldn't even be friends, let alone lovers if they didn't do this.

He knelt before her, inching his body into the gap between her legs.

Her skin was luminous in the light.

He gently held her face as he leaned in to kiss her, while stroking down her neck and across her breasts.

Smoothing around her ribcage, across her back to release her bra, and draw it down and off her arms.

For a minute, he held it, not quite knowing what to do with it.

She broke the kiss to take it from him and toss it into a corner.

He reached for her breasts again, cupping them in his hands, caressing her nipples with his thumbs.

Her skin was soft and smooth, perhaps a little dry.

If there was a second time, he'd rub her with scented oils.

She made a soft noise, and her head fell on his shoulder.

He rubbed his head against hers.

And then she bit him.

He gasped, and his dick leapt against the restraint of his jeans.

For a second or two, he didn't know what to do, then he flicked a nipple, and it was her turn to gasp.

He kissed her mouth as his hands moved lower.

She cupped his chin in her hands and deepened the kiss.

He reached the waistband of her jeans and undid them, but they were tight enough he couldn't get any closer to her.

There's no doubt it's almost impossible to get jeans off in a way that's sexy.

But she leaned back on her elbows, arching her body off the bed.

He snagged the waist and pulled them, bunching around his hands as he took them off her body and cast them aside.

Revealing briefs that matched her bra. Mostly lace. Concealing next to nothing.

He looked up at her, "Norah, were you planning to seduce me?"

"Cheeky boy. I wear undies like this all the time."

"So back at the restaurant when we met, you were wearing your suit of armour and something like this?"

"Yes. Green ones. Didn't you notice them in your bathroom?"

He shook his head, imagining peeling the suit off to reveal them, and groaned.

"And every day, you're dressed all business on the surface, with fripperies like this underneath?"

"Uh-huh."

"Oh my god, you're killing me."

Her chortle became a gasp as he stroked her through the lace.

"I can hardly bear to take them off," he said, slipping his fingers through the leg hole.

She sat up and leaned forward to whisper to him, "you know what?"

"What?" he whispered back.

"Sometimes I wear stockings and suspenders too."

He groaned and dipped his head, "I'm a gonna for sure."

"Just think about that for a moment, while I take your clothes off."

She slid her hands under his jumper, around his back and pulled the jumper up his body, her fingernails lightly grazing his skin as she dragged it over his head.

He smiled at her, not releasing his hold of her, enjoying the sensation of entrapment. Then slid his fingers into her, watching her face as she closed her eyes and sighed.

Her nipples hardened as if calling him, and he obliged, taking one into his mouth and laving it with his tongue.

She groaned, rocked against his hand, and before he could do anything to prolong it, her muscles were clenching his fingers, and she called out a name.

His name.

This time it was his name.

He was surprised she'd orgasmed so quickly.

Maybe because she was older, she knew what she needed. Less inhibited, less concerned about what he expected of her.

Or maybe she'd been thinking about their morning interaction all day.

Primed and ready to go off, so to speak.

Maybe she was ready for more.

He knew he was.

Their eyes met, and she smiled.

Wolfishly. Maybe even predatorily.

While he was basking in the glow of a job well done, she ripped the jumper off his arms and cast it aside.

Holding tight to the waistband of his jeans, she pulled him onto her, then rolled him on his back, and sat on him. Legs either side of his body.

He tried to roll her underneath him, but she was surprisingly strong. And he was a little afraid of hurting her, so he didn't try too hard.

He hoped her plan was to ride him, but he had no idea what she was doing.

And not being in charge, not knowing, was more exciting than he'd expected.

She was like an inhibited Art Nouveau nude oil painting; large breasts, rounded belly, and thick, lush body hair.

Artless, natural.

Fun.

If she was unsure of herself, it didn't show.

She popped the button of his jeans and drew the zip down, releasing his erection.

He watched her as she grasped it, thumb stroking the tip.

His belly clenched and he swallowed, his mind racing with all the possibilities of what might come next.

She bent, slipping her hands into his front pockets, grazing him with her breasts as she did.

Finding his wallet, she opened it up, discovering the condom he'd slipped in the back the day before, because you never know.

She extracted it and tossed his wallet off the bed.

Then patted her chin with the foil wrapper as she watched him watching her.

Slightly unpredictable, completely exhilarating.

She stood up and took her pants off. Standing over him, she squeezed her breasts and ran her hands down her body until she got to the place his fingers had recently been.

"Norah please," he groaned.

She smiled slightly as she lowered herself to kneel over him, watching him as she tore the packet open with her teeth.

Then after a quick glance, rolled the condom onto him.

Pausing for a moment above him, then slowly lowering herself onto him, clenching him for a moment then riding him slowly.

She was sexier than he'd imagined.

He reached for her, but she batted his hands away, letting him watch as she fondled her breasts while she rocked.

She moaned and closed her eyes, then squeaked in surprised when he sat up, wrapped his arms around her body, holding her tight and still as he surged into her.

He was more violent than he'd meant to be, but it seemed she liked it hard and fast because it was next to no time before she was panting and groaning and arching against him.

The sound of her pleasure was so exciting, he couldn't hold himself back any longer, and it was hard to say who was holding who up.

18

It had been so long since Norah had sex with a man, she'd forgotten how powerful it could be, and how fulfilling an orgasm shared with another person was.

She'd been so aroused, the sex and the orgasm was just the right side of painful.

And as she rested her forehead on Daniel's shoulder, she realised she was just about ready to go again.

In the meantime, she leaned into the hardness of his body, enjoying its strength and power; his lean hard abs and powerful chest.

His thighs like tree trunks beneath hers.

The new growth of his beard was a little scratchy against her cheek and snagged in her hair as she rubbed her face against his.

So.

She'd done it.

Had sex with another living human.

And it was good.

But she was now starting to feel the sting of embarrassment about her age and physical condition tainting her warm afterglow.

She should get up.

She should get him a tissue.

She should march him home to his mother.

Should, should, should.

For the moment, she'd give him another five minutes and see what happened.

Not that she could do otherwise, because she was still locked in his arms.

And liking it.

"You don't have a sister do you?" she asked.

He snorted and moved his arm across her back to hold her shoulder against him.

"No."

"What about a jealous ex?"

"No. Why are you asking me this?"

Turning her head, she spoke into his neck, "in the books there's always in interfering sister or ex-girlfriend turning up to ruin everything."

He rubbed her back, "no sisters, no jealous ex-girlfriends, no angry fry pan wielding mothers."

"Angry fry pan wielding mother? I don't think I've read that book."

"Don't worry, I made it up. Just wanted to get ahead of the game."

She snorted, "jealous ex-boyfriends then?"

"No one."

"Why not?"

"Just busy I guess. Long hours at work, renovating my house, reading manga."

"Love Manga."

"I meant to ask how you got to that."

"They're easy to read when you've got things on your mind."

"Anything good lately?"

"Nothing worth telling you about."

"Not worth telling me?" He loosened one arm to scratch his head, "because I'm not worth telling, or because the book's not worth sharing?"

She nudged him with her upper body, and because he wasn't expecting it, he overbalanced backwards. And she fell with him, bracing herself against his body so she didn't head butt him, but brushing his lips with hers as she missed.

He applied a little pressure to her back and lifted his shoulders off the bed to kiss her, slipping his tongue into her mouth as he did.

She was impressed by his ability to hold a semi-sit up with barely a tremble. Curious, she tried to sit up a little further, but he held her firmly against him.

And he was such a good kisser she didn't really mind.

After a time he ended the kiss.

"Should I tell you I'm about ready for round two?" she asked as she stretched, her nipples grazing his chest as she arched her back.

He chuckled, his abdomen jolting her.

"I think I could keep up."

"Another condom?"

"That would mean a trip back to my car."

"Your car? You can't be much of a Risk Manager then."

"Can't be too cocky—" she laughed, and he looked confused until he worked out what he'd said.

"You should be grateful we don't have to go to my place."

"I can't say your place wouldn't be an upgrade on mine."

"What about you? You don't have any here?"

"Uhhh, it hasn't been a priority."

He snorted, "what do you want to do then?"

"I could duck down to the supermarket and buy some."

"How do I know you'll come back to me?"

She frowned, "I live here!"

He laughed, "like I say, how do I know you'll come back to me?"

"I'm not sure I want to go out anyway, but this place is set up for one. I can't even say for sure there's anything useful or helpful in the boxes."

"Would you like some help sorting it out?"

"Sorting it out? Why would I?"

He scratched his head, "it's just that you said you couldn't face opening them. Maybe it will be easier if there's someone else here with you."

Norah looked over her shoulder, and out the bedroom door at the wall of boxes.

After opening a couple earlier, she was more curious about what was in them now.

But it would it help if he was with her?

Or was he curious about what was in them? About Nick.

It didn't really matter.

In a way, opening the boxes was like having sex.

It had to be done so she could move on.

Would it be better or worse with him?

Depended whether he was a "disinterested observer," probably easier for him to tell her to get rid of things than Mariel.

And then she remembered again, "but you said you had plans."

"Sprung. Doesn't matter. I'd rather stay."

Norah checked her watch, "then I should definitely get some wine, some condoms and something to eat."

"Why don't I shop, and let you get started on the boxes?"

Norah grinned, "maybe a shower first."

Though it was quite some time before they got out of the shower.

19

Daniel found himself humming as he walked around the late-night supermarket.

Marial's birthday party had proved more valuable than he'd expected.

And after seeing what wasn't in Norah's cupboards, and the amount of energy she'd expended on him in the last couple of hours...

He paused at the vegetable section. He'd make her a stir-fry, or some soup, or maybe a salad if she didn't have the right cookware.

She looked like she could do with a decent meal.

The memory of her riding him was so much more exciting than he'd imagined his tram surfing superhero could be.

Was that really only yesterday?

He couldn't help imagining peeling off her suit to reveal the beautiful underwear she'd chosen, knowing it would be him doing the peeling, and felt himself harden.

How was it possible she was so much more exciting than the last woman he'd dated.

Perhaps it was the sense that there was more to Norah than you saw on the surface, and that other chick was all surface and no substance.

Though whether substance was something you grew into as you lived, or just what Norah was like, was a question for another day.

Not to mention why he hadn't noticed depth as something missing in the first place.

And after a few orgasms with her, he was still horny. And curious.

Not yet ready to walk away.

Unlike the last woman he'd slept with, he wanted to know more about Norah.

Why didn't she let her phone ring?

Why was she such a mess?

Why did she wear sexy undies that matched? Did she have any daggy old plain ones?

He wanted to see all of them.

He realised he was fondling a yellow pepper and put it in his basket.

As he turned away, the flick of a woman's hair caught his eye, and she smiled over her shoulder at him.

It took a fraction of a second to realise he could have her up against a wall if he wanted to. And slightly less to decide he didn't want to.

Right now he just wanted to get back to Norah.

He turned away to look at the spring onions.

Maybe Norah fascinated him because he couldn't tell at a glance what she was thinking.

Her resting bitch face was impeccable, and he couldn't read her at all.

Despite her mini-meltdown, she didn't blurt out everything that was on her mind. If he wanted to know something, he had to ask her, and she edited her reply.

She was like an open book with half the pages missing.

So.

He was horny, curious, and invested.

But, in some weird way he couldn't define, completely relaxed about it.

He picked up a small piece of beef.

Though he suspected he'd be a lot less relaxed if another bloke turned up and started sniffing around her.

Which surprised him.

He'd been more worried about her becoming too attached to him than the reverse, but was it possible she'd be the one avoiding him.

Well yes, because she didn't look at her phone, but for real?

Though she'd given him her door key, so she would at least welcome him back with wine.

And condoms.

A big box of condoms.

The biggest box of condoms.

And a bitter-sweet dark chocolate brownie thing, because he thought she might like that better than milk chocolate.

He took his shopping through the self-service checkout. For some reason, a little embarrassed about the condoms, not want to take them past the young woman at the checkout.

How nuts was that?

And since when did he want to make a woman happy anyway?

Looked like he might already be in too deep.

He paused outside her door.

"Let yourself in," she'd said, but even so it felt peculiar.

He eased the door open to a dark and silent apartment.

He was afraid something had happened, and ease the tension, called out, "honey, I'm home."

But as he listened to the words come out of his mouth, he realised that actually, his home might well be wherever she was.

Her voice drifted out of the darkness, "that's good timing Colonel, the light blew, and I wondered if you might change the globe?"

He shut the door behind him, and as his eyes adjusted, he realised it wasn't completely dark or silent.

Norah was sitting on the floor in the middle of stacked up piles of stuff.

She turned to look at him, ignoring the pile of crockery she'd knocked over as it fell with a crash.

And of course, she had an adorable smear of dirt across her cheek.

She reached a hand out towards him, "give me a hand up?"

"Always," he said, and pulled her into a kiss.

Alexandria Blaelock writes stories, some of them for *Ellery Queen's Mystery Magazine* and *Pulphouse Fiction Magazine.*

She's also written four self-help books applying business techniques to personal matters like getting dressed, cleaning house, and feeding your friends.

As a recovering Project Manager, she's probably too fond of sticking to plan. She lives in a forest because she enjoys birdsong, the scent of gum leaves and the sun on her face. When not telecommuting to parallel universes from her Melbourne based imagination, she watches K-dramas, talks to animals, and drinks Campari.
At the same time.

Discover more at www.alexandriablaelock.com.